Contents

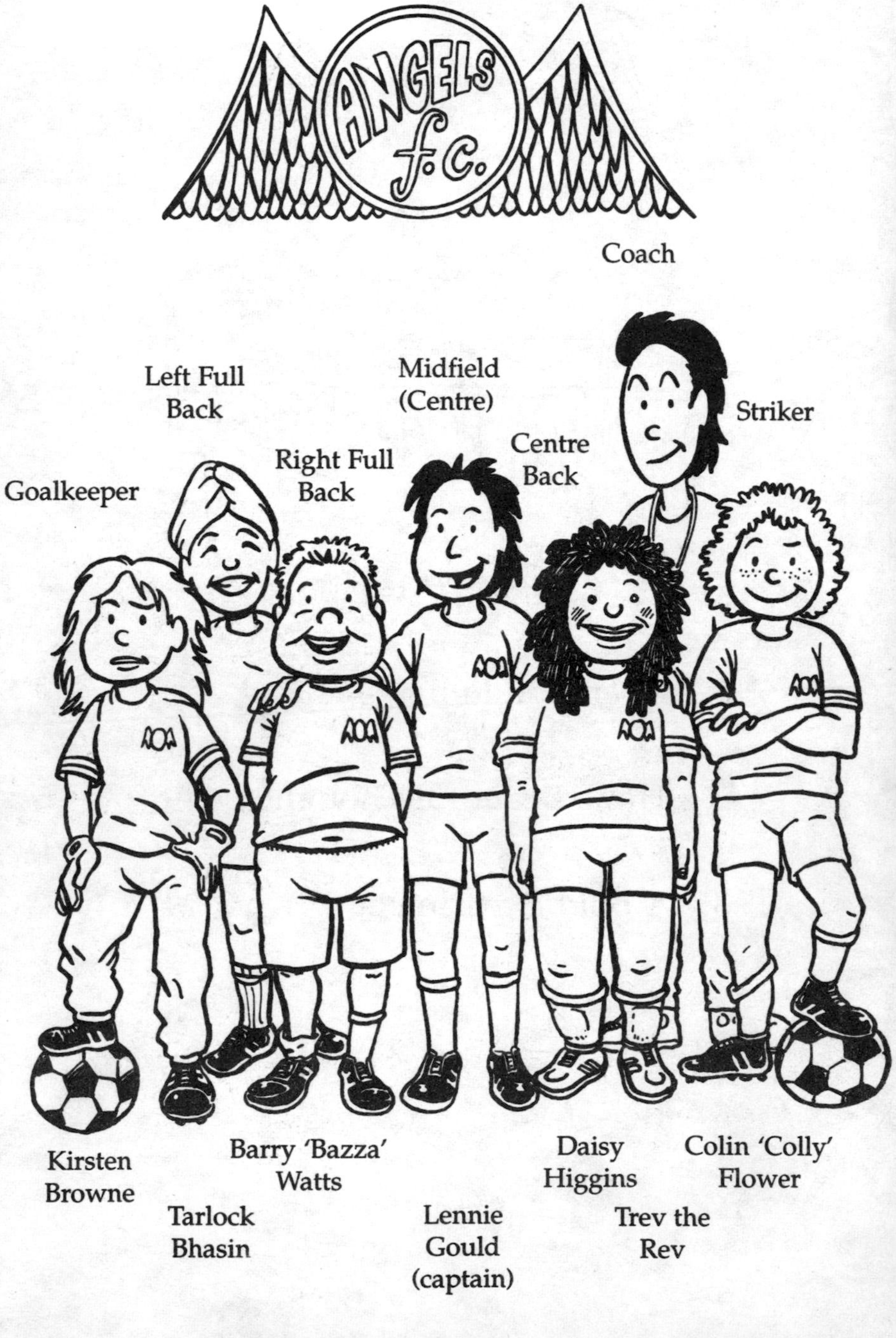

Coach

Left Full
Back

Midfield
(Centre)

Striker

Right Full
Back

Centre
Back

Goalkeeper

Kirsten
Browne

Barry 'Bazza'
Watts

Daisy
Higgins

Colin 'Colly'
Flower

Tarlock
Bhasin

Lennie
Gould
(captain)

Trev the
Rev

Substitute

Midfield
(Centre)

Centre
Back

Substitute

Midfield
(Right)

Striker

Midfield
(Left)

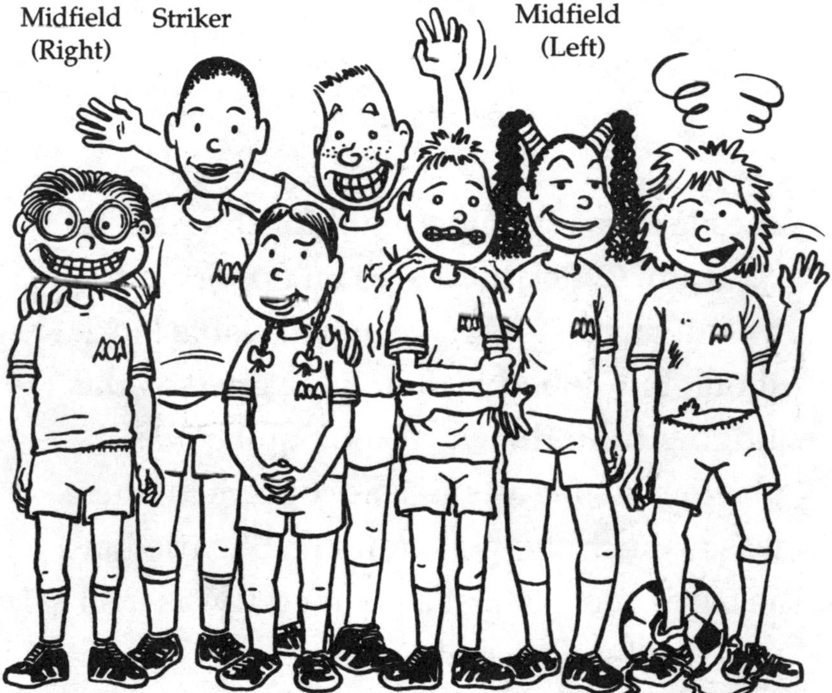

Mick
Ryall

Jonjo
Rix

Lulu
Squibb

Jeremy
Emery

Rhoda
O'Neill

Lionel
Murgatroyd

Ricky
King

1

Operation Lulu!

Tuesday was training night for the Angels FC team. Officially, it was an opportunity to try out tactics and have an enjoyable kick-about, but nobody could have guessed this judging from the way Lulu Squibb was playing. As far as she was concerned, there was no such thing as training. She tried just as hard, and got just as wound up, as if she was playing in a real match!

Whirling into a tackle, Lulu whipped the ball from the toes of Lionel Murgatroyd, the

Angels' regular substitute, and raced off down the pitch. Tricking her way past Mick Ryall with a nifty body swerve, she closed in on goal.

Another couple of steps, she thought, and then…

"Ooomph!"

Just as Lulu was preparing to let fly with a shot hard enough to break the net, Daisy Higgins looped one of her long legs round from behind and tripped her up.

"Daisy rotten Higgins!" screamed Lulu, leaping to her feet. "I'll knock your block off!"

Only the fierce shriek of a whistle stopped Lulu carrying out her threat.

"Calm down, Lulu, calm down!" cried the team's coach, Trevor Rowe, who was refereeing the practice game as usual. Placing the ball at Lulu's feet, he murmured, "Concentrate. Come on, they're not looking. You can hit them with a quick free kick."

"Good thinking, Trev," said Lulu, seeing just what he meant. Most of the Angels' defenders were looking the other way.

She glanced to her left. Colin 'Colly' Flower was in the clear. If she whipped it out to him quickly he'd have a clear run on goal.

She drew her foot back…only to see the ball disappear as Jeremy Emery ran past and flicked it away.

Lulu's eyes flashed. "You big prune! He kicked the ball away. Book him for time-wasting, Trev!"

"Lulu, it's not a proper match."

"Book him for having dirty knees, then! Book him for having a tongue-twister name like Jeremy Emery! I don't care, just book him!"

Trev wagged a gentle finger in the centre-back's direction. "Fair play, Jeremy. Remember the Angels' code: 'Angels on and off the field'!"

"He'll remember it if I get my hands on him!" yelled Lulu, going red in the face. "I'll turn him into a real angel!"

Colly Flower hurried over to replace the ball. "Get ready, Lulu. I'll lay it off for you. You can take a shot."

Still seething, Lulu stepped back five or six paces to give herself a good run in. Trev's whistle blew. Just as he'd promised, Colly slid the ball invitingly to the side. But just as Lulu was going to surge forward and smack it with all her might, the large shape of Jonjo Rix stepped squarely in front of her.

"Get out of my way, you great lummock!" she yelled.

Jonjo showed no sign of doing what he was told. In fact, as Lulu moved to her right to try to get round him, Jonjo moved to the right as well. She skipped to her left. Immediately, Jonjo went that way too, still blocking her path.

With a snarl of rage, Lulu tried the only thing she could think of. Dropping to her knees, she tried scrambling between Jonjo's

legs. But, as she got half-way through, Jonjo
snapped his legs together like a vice. She
couldn't move forward – and she couldn't
move back either!

"Let me go, you big elephant! Foul, Trev!
Obstruction! Red card!"

Even as she was yelling, though, Lulu
was looping her hands around Jonjo's
ankles. With a furious tug, she yanked them
forward.

"Aaaarrggh!" cried the hefty Angels' striker in surprise, as his feet lifted off the ground and he found himself toppling over.

Almost before he hit the ground, Lulu had leapt free and was jumping on top of him.

"You great lump! I'll teach you to get in my way! I'll put your lights out!"

"Peace!" giggled Jonjo, unable to keep a straight face.

Trev gave a long loud blast on his whistle. "Full time! End of Operation Lulu!"

Eleven pairs off hands lifted Lulu into the air and began to carry her back to the changing rooms.

Operation Lulu? It had been a set-up!

"Well everybody," said Trev once they were all seated. "Operation Lulu seemed to work spectacularly well."

Lulu looked up. All the Angels players were grinning broadly. "Operation Lulu?" she asked. "What do you mean?"

"Trev told us to annoy you deliberately," said Lennie Gould, the team's captain.

Lulu glared at Trev. "Why? You know I get annoyed if I'm annoyed!"

"And so do the team we're playing on Saturday – Ashley Wanderers," said Trev.

"The team your cousin Roysten plays in goal for, remember?" added Tarlock Bhasin.

"Of course I remember," said Lulu. "That's why I always play well against them. There's nothing I like better than banging a couple of goals past Roysten."

"And it's because you always play well against them that they try to get you to lose your temper," said Daisy Higgins. "Remember last time?"

Lulu nodded. "Roysten wiped his filthy goalkeeper's glove on my shirt, so I gave him a mouthful – of mud." She hooted with laughter. "He nearly swallowed it!"

Trev was serious, though. "But what also

happened was that the referee booked you, and I had to bring you off before you were sent off. That's why we held Operation Lulu tonight – to give you some practice at not losing your temper!"

"And, er…how did I do?" asked Lulu, quietly.

"Terrible!" they all shouted.

Lulu gave an embarrassed smile. "Really? Crumbs. And you didn't even do the thing that annoys me most of all!"

"What's that?" called Bazza Watts. "I'll try it next practice night!"

"I'm not saying," replied Lulu. She gave Bazza a glare. "But you'd know if you did it. I'd go into orbit – and so would you!"

Trev cut the debate short. "Well, if you don't want me bringing you off again this Saturday, Lulu, you'd better hope you've used up all your temper for the week."

"I won't let you down, Trev," Lulu told the coach a few minutes later, after she'd got changed and was on her way out.

Trev smiled. "Think beautiful thoughts. That's what I do."

"Think beautiful thoughts," echoed Lulu. "Right." She opened the door, then groaned. "Oh, yes. I'll be going straight to Ashley's ground on Saturday, Trev. And you'll never

guess – I'll be with Roysten. Mum and Dad
have gone away for a few days and they've
arranged for me to stay with him and Uncle
Hubert."

"With Roysten?" called Lennie Gould as
he overheard. "Well, just make sure he
doesn't find out what really makes you lose
your temper, or you can bet he'll try it
during the game."

"Don't worry, he won't find out," said
Lulu. "That's my secret – and it's staying
that way!

Pushing through the door, she went outside – only to bump straight into her cousin Roysten. He was leaning against the changing-room wall.

"I've come to meet you," he said miserably.

"Oh, how kind," said Lulu. "Or did Uncle Hubert make you?"

"He made me, of course," growled Roysten. His face suddenly broke into a smile. "But now I'm glad he did."

A nasty feeling hit Lulu.

"Why?" she asked.

He pointed to the open changing-room window above his head.

"Because if I hadn't, I wouldn't have heard you talking about your secret, would I? And now I've got until Saturday to find out what it is!"

2

Think Beautiful Thoughts

Roysten lived on the outskirts of town, in a large, rambling and extremely old house. It was so old, it was said to have at least one hidden tunnel. Lulu could well believe it. If the tunnel began somewhere in the garden it would be the best-hidden tunnel in the world because, apart from a large mown square of grass in the centre, the rest of the garden resembled a jungle.

"Gardening? Bah!" Uncle Hubert would say. "Complete waste of time. I've got much more important things to do!"

Exactly what the important things were that Uncle Hubert spent his time on, Lulu wasn't too sure. He was a scientist of some sort, and had his own laboratory in the basement of the house. Lulu had never seen inside it. The closest she'd ever got was when she had wandered down into the basement on one of her visits and had seen the solid wooden door with its large 'Danger! No Entry! Keep Out!' signs.

Just in case she was in any doubt Uncle Hubert mentioned it the moment they sat down for supper.

"It's lovely to have you here to stay, Lulu," he said, cheerfully. "Make yourself at home. Regard the house as your own. Go anywhere you like..." – then his bushy eyebrows dipped and he fixed Lulu with his wild professor's look – "...except into the basement. Do not, repeat, NOT, go down into the basement. I am on the verge of a great discovery, one I've been hunting for for years and years – and I do not want my equipment wrecked by a whistling football!"

Roysten was sitting on the other side of the table. "I don't suppose Lulu will want to play football," he sneered. "She won't want to give away any of her secrets."

"Ah, yes," said Uncle Hubert to Lulu. "Roysten told me your team are playing his on Saturday."

"That's right, Uncle Hubert. Though one thing's no secret. The fact that Angels are going to give Ashley the biggest whacking— owwww!"

Lulu gave a sudden yelp as Roysten suddenly gave *her* a sharp kick on the ankle under the cover of the table.

"Anything wrong, my dear?" asked Uncle Hubert.

Lulu was about to tell him exactly what was wrong when, just in time, Trev's words came floating into her mind. Think beautiful thoughts! It worked. Instead of yelling, Lulu contented herself with thinking the beautiful thought of thumping the ball straight into Roysten's ugly mug during their coming match.

"Nothing wrong at all, Uncle Hubert," she said, sweetly – but made sure she kept her ankles well out of the way for the rest of supper.

Keeping completely out of Roysten's way over the next few days was a lot harder, though. His tactic was to pop up when she least expected him and try something to see if it made her lose her temper.

He suddenly appeared behind her when she was at the top of the stairs next morning.

"Does an elbow in the ribs do it, I wonder?" he scowled, before giving her one.

Sent off balance, Lulu would have fallen headlong down the stairs if she hadn't leapt onto the bannisters and slid down instead.

"Watch it, you!" snapped Lulu. Then Trev's advice came into mind again, making her think of Roysten sitting in a puddle as she dribbled rings round him. "I mean, silly me! Bashing your elbow with my ribs like that. Is it all right?"

On Thursday morning Lulu tried to stay out of Roysten's way by not getting up at all, but pretending to be asleep. It didn't work. As she was lying in bed the door creaked open and a feather on a stick came stretching through and began to tickle the soles of her feet.

"Gerroutofit!!" she yelled.

"Is that your secret, I wonder?" called Roysten.

"You'll find out if I get hold of you!" Leaping out of bed, Lulu chased after her cousin – only to be tripped up by the length of string he'd stretched across the doorway.

"Aaarrggh!"

Landing nose first, Lulu hurtled across the polished floor as if she'd been fouled by an expert. She leapt up, her fists clenched.

"Come 'ere, Roysten! I'm going to…" – but once again Trev's words came into mind – "…score against you on Saturday," she trilled, sweetly. "You see if I don't."

Now it was Roysten's turn to get mad.

"All right. I've tried the gentle things. I've tried ankle-tapping. I've tried nudging you in the ribs. I've tried tickling and I've tried tripping. So if none of those are your secret, then I can see it's time I turned nasty!"

Lulu sighed as Roysten stormed off downstairs. Trev's advice had really helped, and she had done well. Sooner or later, though, Roysten was going to do the thing that really sent her wild. It was so obvious, she couldn't understand why he hadn't tried it yet.

So how could she stay out of his way for the rest of the day? The idea came to her as she looked out of the window and saw the mown patch of grass in the middle of Uncle Hubert's jungle garden.

Lulu strolled to the top of the stairs. "Hey, Roysten! How about a kick-about in the garden? Three goals and in."

3

A Bold Experiment

Lulu set up a goal just in front of the most overgrown part of the garden.

"You want to go in goal first, Roysten?" she asked.

Roysten agreed. "OK. Maybe your secret is that you get really mad when your best shots are saved by a brilliant keeper!"

To start with, Lulu hit a couple of gentle shots that even Uncle Hubert could have saved. Then she tried six in a row that were all deliberately wide, so that Roysten had to

scramble amongst the overgrown bushes
behind their goal to get the ball back. It was
immediately after his sixth
retrieval, as he stood in
goal puffing and
panting, that Lulu put
her plan into action.

Taking careful aim,
she hammered the ball
high over Roysten's
head and into the
deepest part of the
undergrowth.

Her cousin groaned.
"You can get that one."

Lulu cheerfully plunged into the jungle.
Deeper and deeper she went, reaching parts
that looked as though they hadn't been
touched in centuries. She found the ball, not
far away from the tall tree at which she'd
aimed. And then...she went even further

into the undergrowth, found the bushiest
bush ever – and sat down.

Perfect! What a plan! All she had to do
was hide here for the rest of the day and
Roysten couldn't annoy her or try any other
trick to discover her secret.

She didn't answer when Roysten,
sounding far away, called, "Lulu! Haven't
you found it yet?" Soon, she hoped, he
would give up waiting and go away.

That was the flaw in her plan. Roysten didn't go away. She'd only been in her hiding place for a few minutes when she heard him crunching through the undergrowth towards her. "I've just worked out what you're up to. You're hiding from me. Well it won't work!"

Lulu decided it was time to move. Crawling on all fours, she pushed her way further into the jungle.

Cra-ack!

At the sound of splintering wood, Lulu felt something give way beneath her hand. Looking down she saw a rotten wooden trapdoor – and, beneath it, there was a gaping hole...

"It's one of the hidden tunnels," gasped Lulu. "It must be!"

She pulled away the rest of the mouldy trapdoor and hopped down. It *was* a tunnel! She could see a square of light at the far end. Perhaps it led back into the house? If it did, Roysten would never find her!

Lulu crept towards the light – and discovered why it was square-shaped. It was oozing out from the four sides of a small door, with a rusty iron handle. Lulu held her breath and pushed. The door squeaked open to reveal…a room full of benches and cupboards, test-tubes and bubbling glass containers. She'd come out through a fake panel in the wall of Uncle Hubert's laboratory!

There was no sign of Uncle Hubert.
Perhaps she could just take a little look
around? Throwing her pigtails over her
shoulder, Lulu crept through the gap and
into the brightly lit laboratory...

"Gotcha!"

As she felt her pigtails given a mighty tug
from behind, Lulu jumped wildly into the
air. She shook her head like a maniac. It was
no good. Roysten, who had found the
passage and followed her down, still had
her pigtails tightly in his hands. He tugged
again. The effect was dramatic.

"Let go!" screamed Lulu. "I'll mangle you! I'll pulverise you! I'll tear you limb from limb if you don't LET GO OF MY HAIR!"

Behind her, Roysten whooped in triumph. "That's your secret! I bet it is! You can't stand having your pigtails pulled!" He gave them another hard tug, to test his theory.

Lulu shot backwards. Whirling round to give him a thump, she accidentally knocked a bubbling jar of green liquid off Uncle Hubert's work-bench and onto the floor. Other equipment clattered over. Lulu spun again.

35

This time she managed to wrench herself
free, but as she did so, she thumped against
the bench, causing a huge test-tube full of
red gunge to smash on the floor and mix
with the green stuff.

"It *is* your secret!" crowed Roysten,
delightedly.

"All right, now you know!" cried Lulu.
Her cousin was edging nearer, his hands
outstretched.

Lulu backed away – into the red and green mixture on the floor. Suddenly, it felt as if the soles of her trainers were made of ice, only a thousand times more slippery. Shooting off backwards, she slithered into a tall cupboard. Down it came with a crash.

"Oh, no!" groaned Lulu.

Her secret discovered, the laboratory wrecked. What else could go wrong?

Only one thing. At that very moment, the laboratory door opened and in stepped Uncle Hubert.

4

Eureka!

"What have you done!" bellowed Uncle
Hubert, bristling with rage.

"I found a tunnel," wailed Lulu. "I didn't
know it led into here. Then Roysten came
up behind me and pulled my—"

"Roysten?" growled Uncle Hubert,
looking around. "Roysten isn't here."

He was right. Roysten wasn't there. While
her eyes had been on Uncle Hubert's arrival,
Roysten must have dived back into the tunnel
and shut the fake door behind him. She

couldn't even see where it was!

"Well, he was," Lulu stormed, the words tumbling out. "He pulled my hair so I swung round to sock him one but I missed and hit one of your jars instead so I had another swing but I missed again and hit a test-tube and then I saw him coming for me so I tried to get away and I slipped and knocked the cupboard over and…and…" She looked at Uncle Hubert's furious face. "…You're not happy, are you?"

"No, I am not happy!" yelled Uncle Hubert. "And if I'm not happy, then I'm going to make quite sure that you're not happy either."

"H-how?"

"By making you clear this mess up on Saturday instead of playing football!"

Lulu picked up the laboratory telephone and dialled Trev's number.

"No need for great explanations," said Uncle Hubert, almost breathing down her neck. "Just tell him that you can't play in the match."

Lulu's mind was in a whirl. She'd tried her hardest to get Uncle Hubert to change his mind. "I can't let them down. They'll be expecting me to turn up."

"Then you can telephone and say you won't be there!" had been his stern reply.

So that's what she was doing – calling

Trev to give him the bad news. As the phone rang at the other end, Lulu thought frantically. She simply *had* to play on Saturday. Somehow she'd have to get Uncle Hubert to change his mind between now and the game. So, what she definitely didn't want to do now was tell Trev that she couldn't play. He'd go straight off and give her place to their substitute, Lionel Murgatroyd. But telling Trev she couldn't play on Saturday was exactly what Uncle Hubert *did* want her to say! What on earth could she do?

At the other end the ringing stopped. There was a short pause and then an electronic voice said, "This is St Jude's Church. I'm sorry, but Trevor Rowe isn't here at the moment. Please leave your message after the beep."

Lulu's eyes lit up. "It's an answering machine!" She went to put the phone down. "I'd better leave it, eh?"

"Leave it?" snapped Uncle Hubert. "Quite right. You will leave your message."

Lulu sighed. There was no way out. "Hello, Trev," she said. "It's Lulu. I just rang to say that I can't play..."

42

That was when she had her brainwave. As a whirring sound came from the other end of the line she added, "in goal on Saturday!"

She clicked the phone down with hope in her heart. It was a perfect solution. All it needed was for Trev to realise that, as Lulu never had played in goal, a message from her saying that she *couldn't* play in goal meant that she *could* play in any other position!

On Saturday morning, Roysten set off for the game with a smug look on his face.

"Look on the bright side," he sneered, "if you were playing you wouldn't stay on the pitch for long. Now I know your secret, I'd get you sent off in the first minute!"

Feeling dismal, Lulu went down to the basement. She'd thought and thought about how she might escape from Uncle Hubert but still hadn't come up with an idea. But then, as she entered the laboratory, she saw a way.

Uncle Hubert was already there. He'd cleaned up the broken glass and was unloading new test-tubes and jars from a very tall walk-in cupboard. What's more, it was a cupboard with a lock – and he'd left the key in it! That had to be the solution. She would lock him in, go off to play in the match – and then worry about what would happen to her afterwards.

Lulu waited until Uncle Hubert went into the cupboard again. Then, creeping round by the bench so that he couldn't see her, Lulu got nearer and nearer until…she slipped once again in the patch of red and green gunge that was in a puddle on the floor!

"Waaaahhhh!"

Once again it felt as though she was skating on incredibly slippery ice. Struggling to stay upright, she shot across the room and straight into Uncle Hubert as he came out of the cupboard.

"Ooooompph!"

"It's that stuff!" cried Lulu as they untangled themselves. "That's what made me slip before!"

Bending to inspect the puddle, Uncle Hubert dabbed at it with his finger. He pulled out a pair of tweezers and tested the edges. Then, to Lulu's surprise – and to Uncle Hubert's joy – he peeled it up from the floor in one large jelly-like piece.

"Amazing! Wonderful!" cried Uncle Hubert. "I've been searching for this for years!" He took Lulu in his arms and waltzed her round the laboratory a couple of times, before asking her anxiously, "How did you manage it? Try to remember, Lulu, it's vitally important!"

Lulu knew exactly how she'd done it. "It was the jar of bubbling green stuff which got mixed up with the test-tube of red gunge. But – why? You mean you actually *want* to make slippery blobs like that?"

"Oh, yes!" cried Uncle Hubert. "Look at it!" He dropped the blob back onto the floor. "It's as slippery as ice on top, and although it sticks firmly to the floor, it can be peeled off easily."

"But what use is it?"

"It means no more bad backs for people who want to lift heavy things, that's what! You just spread this mixture on the floor, slide the heavy object to where you want it, then peel the blob up and throw it away. Brilliant!"

Humming delightedly, Uncle Hubert filled dozens of test-tubes with green liquid and red gunge. "Wonderful! Marvellous!" he said to himself. Then, looking at Lulu looking at him, a big beam crossed his face.

"Are you still here? I thought you had a football match!"

Lulu's eyes lit up. "You mean...? Yes, I have!"

She darted for the door – then stopped. Uncle Hubert's back was turned. It would only take a moment, and it could be the answer to her other problem...

Moments later she was on her way.

Behind her, Uncle Hubert was so excited about his new discovery that he didn't even notice that one of his test-tubes full of slippery stuff had disappeared.

"...Can't play =Bzzzt=!

5

Tug-of-War!

Lulu reached the ground with five minutes to spare. As she raced across to the changing rooms she saw that most of the Angels players were already out on the pitch.

She met a surprised Trev at the changing-room door. "But – the message on my answering machine...you said you couldn't play!"

"I said I couldn't play *in goal*," said Lulu. "I was in a spot of bother. You were supposed to work out that it meant I *could* play in my usual position."

"No," said Trev firmly. "The message definitely said, 'I can't play.' That's all. I remember because it was right at the end of the tape."

"The whirring noise," cried an agonised Lulu, recalling the sound she'd heard while she was on the phone. "That must have been your tape running out. You didn't get the last part of my message!"

The Angels coach sighed. "I'm sorry, Lulu. When I thought you couldn't play I told Lionel Murgatroyd he'd be taking your place. He's out on the pitch now, excited as anything. You'll have to be substitute, Lulu. I'll put you on in the second half."

Lionel was the Angels' regular substitute. He hardly ever got to start a game. Lulu was pleased for him, but – no, not in her place!

"Sub?" yelled Lulu. "Sub! I can run rings round Ashley Wanderers, you said so yourself."

"Only if you can keep your temper."

"I can," said Lulu, desperately. "I know I can."

"I don't reckon so," came a voice from the door. It was Roysten, changed and on his way out to the pitch, his massive goalkeeping gloves under his arm. "Because I know your little secret, don't I, Lulu? And so do the rest of my team now!"

As Roysten trotted off laughing, Trev shook his head. "That's it, then. Sorry, Lulu. Substitute you'll have to be – and I'm not even sure I'll be able to risk bringing you on at all."

The match began with Lulu fuming on the touchline.

It quickly became obvious that the team were missing her in midfield. Lionel Murgatroyd was enthusiastic, but not much else. He seemed to spend most of his time chasing the ball rather than winning it. Ashley repeatedly launched attacks through the middle of the field that Lulu's tigerish tackling would have stopped.

Then, when the Angels did manage to get forward themselves, they found Roysten playing brilliantly in the Ashley goal with every cross and shot seeming to land slap-bang in the middle of his huge gloves.

"Will I get on in the second half?" Lulu asked at half-time, with the Angels lucky that the score was still 0–0.

"Maybe," said Trev. "Let's see how it goes."

It didn't go well.

As another Angels cross was plucked out of the air by Roysten, Lulu's cousin threw the ball quickly into midfield with Lionel Murgatroyd stranded miles out of position.

Surging forward in numbers, the Ashley players combined well. A quick one-two, a measured through-ball, and within moments their striker was banging the ball past Kirsten Browne and into the Angels' net.

1–0 to Ashley!

On the touchline, Lulu pleaded, "Trev, put me on!"

Trev looked undecided. "I don't know, Lulu. If you lose your temper..."

I WILL NOT LOSE MY TEMPER!

"Er...let's leave it a little longer, eh?" Trev left it a little longer... and a little longer... until, with just over five minutes to go and Angels no closer to scoring the equaliser, he finally said, "OK, Lulu. Get ready. You're going on."

"Brilliant! I'll just warm up."

But instead of haring up and down the touchline, as substitutes normally do before they come on, Lulu raced only as far as the sports bag she'd brought out with her from the changing room. She knelt there for a few moments, then leapt to her feet.

"Ready, Trev. Let me at 'em!"

As the Angels' winger, Mick Ryall, won a corner on the right, the referee waved Lulu on. She raced immediately into the heart of the Ashley penalty area. Roysten saw her coming.

"Well, well," he said, as Lulu planted herself right under his nose on the goal-line. "Look who it isn't. Pigtail Patsy. Maybe I'll just give 'em a little tweak."

"Don't even think about it, Roysten," growled Lulu.

"Whadda-madda-den? Will it make baby scream and shout, will it?"

"Pull my pigtails and you'll see what it does," snarled Lulu, not moving away.

"Pull 'em?" said Roysten. "Thanks for the invitation. I think I will."

Leaning forward, he wrapped one huge goalkeeper's glove around each pigtail and pulled hard.

An instant later, Roysten found himself holding nothing but thin air.

"You'll have to do better than that," laughed Lulu.

Roysten tried again. But again the same thing happened. He wrapped a glove round each pigtail, pulled – and once again found them slithering out of his grasp.

"What have you put on them?" he squawked.

"Ask Uncle Hubert," laughed Lulu. "It's his new wonder invention. I smothered my pigtails with a test-tube full just before I came on!"

Laughing in triumph, she ran back to her

usual spot whenever the Angels took a
corner – on the edge of the penalty area. Out
on the right, Mick Ryall swung the kick
across. Normally he was very accurate, but
this time he put it too close to the Ashley
goal.

"Keeper's!" bellowed Roysten.

As she saw him leap towards the ball, a
sudden thought struck Lulu. She'd put
Uncle Hubert's slippery stuff on her pigtails,
and Roysten had tried to grab those same
pigtails... Maybe Roysten's gloves...?

She raced back into the penalty area, arriving just as the ball thumped into Roysten's gloves – and slithered out again! As it dropped at her feet, Lulu simply had to tap it into the net for the equaliser!

Angels 1 – Ashley 1!

The game restarted. Immediately, Lulu whirled into a ruck of Ashley players to try to win the ball back.

"Grab them pigtails!" yelled somebody. "It drives her wild!"

Hands reached out, but all slid off harmlessly. Lulu, able to concentrate on what she was doing, won the ball with a crunching tackle. Breaking free, she looked up. In the Ashley goal a mystified Roysten, still trying to work out what had happened, was inspecting his gloves. He wasn't even aware that they'd kicked off again.

Without a second thought, Lulu thumped the ball towards the Ashley goal.

"Roysten!"

The shouts from his team-mates caused Roysten to look up. Lulu groaned. She hadn't hit her shot terribly well and her cousin would now have plenty of time to gather it.

As the ball bounced up to him, Roysten held out his hands to catch it. No sooner had it landed in his gloves, though, than it squirted out again. He tried to pick it up again, but once more it shot out of his gloves – this time over his shoulder.

Roysten turned. The ball was trickling towards his goal. In a panic he dived onto it.

The coating of Uncle Hubert's slippery solution on his gloves worked again. Like a round bar of soap, the ball shot out from beneath Roysten's hands and into the Ashley net for an own goal!

Angels 2 – Ashley 1!

As the final whistle blew, Roysten made a beeline for the referee. "Foul, ref! She doctored my gloves!"

The referee shook his head. "No, she didn't. I was watching very carefully. You tried to pull her hair. You were lucky she didn't complain, or I'd have sent you off."

"Me?" yelled Roysten. "She's the one who should have been sent off. She's deadly!"

Lulu laughed. "Me? Oh, Roysten – I'm just a 'slip' of a girl!"